... but I'm

...ming of sunshine and
...ummer days and ice-cream
sundaes . . . yum! Dreaming can
brighten up even the greyest
days, and, for me at least,
scoffing ice cream has exactly
the same effect!!! I thought it
would be fun to combine the
two themes in a fab freebie mini-book, and that's where
the idea of *Ice cream and Dreams* started. Chase away
the blues – curl up with something sweet to eat and read
my brand-new Cat and Mouse story. (If you haven't come
across Cat and Mouse before, read more about them in my
fab book *Lucky Star*, which is out in paperback this month!)

Want more to read? Dip into a chapter from my next book,
Ginger Snaps on page 23, and get to know new characters
Ginger, Shannon, Emily . . . and cool, crazy Sam. *Ginger
Snaps* will be on sale in July, so not long to wait!

Tell your friends too – and get together for a fab, ice-
cream-themed sleepover . . . try out our cool quizzes,
make your own lush ice-cream sundaes, then just relax
and dream. Sweet 'n' cool, just like ice cream . . . what
could be better?

Love,

Cat

Books by Cathy Cassidy

Look out for

cathy cassidy

Ice cream and Dreams

PUFFIN

PUFFIN BOOKS

Published by the Penguin Group
Penguin Books Ltd, 80 Strand, London WC2R 0RL, England
Penguin Group (USA) Inc., 375 Hudson Street, New York, New York 10014, USA
Penguin Group (Canada), 90 Eglinton Avenue East, Suite 700, Toronto,
Ontario, Canada M4P 2Y3 (a division of Pearson Penguin Canada Inc.)
Penguin Ireland, 25 St Stephen's Green, Dublin 2, Ireland
(a division of Penguin Books Ltd)
Penguin Group (Australia), 250 Camberwell Road, Camberwell,
Victoria 3124, Australia (a division of Pearson Australia Group Pty Ltd)
Penguin Books India Pvt Ltd, 11 Community Centre,
Panchsheel Park, New Delhi – 110 017, India
Penguin Group (NZ), 67 Apollo Drive, Rosedale, North Shore 0632,
New Zealand (a division of Pearson New Zealand Ltd)
Penguin Books (South Africa) (Pty) Ltd, 24 Sturdee Avenue,
Rosebank, Johannesburg 2196, South Africa

Penguin Books Ltd, Registered Offices: 80 Strand, London WC2R 0RL, England

puffinbooks.com

First published 2008
1

Copyright © Cathy Cassidy, 2008
Made and printed in England by Clays Ltd, St Ives plc

ISBN: 978-0-141-32456-2

Contents

wish on a star

Some of you may have read Cathy Cassidy's
latest gorgeous novel, LUCKY STAR, which picks up
on the story of Mouse, one of the characters in
Cathy's very first novel, DIZZY.

In LUCKY STAR, Mouse meets a girl called Cat from the
other side of the tracks. Trouble seems to follow the unlikely
pair around, but sometimes their friendship
helps to keep them out of it too.

**Read on for a very special, exclusive extra
scene, where Mouse surprises Cat with a
birthday treat to remember . . .**

Mr Brown just didn't get it, really, when I asked to do my work experience week at the planetarium.

'Are you planning on being an astronaut?' he asked, smirking. 'An astronomer? An inter-planetary graffiti vandal?'

That hurt, a little. The graffiti incident was ages ago. I am a reformed character now.

'I'm interested in the stars, Sir,' I told him.

Mr Brown nodded. My classmates had asked for work experience as garage mechanics and plumbers, with the more ambitious kids signing up to work at the leisure centre, but Mr Brown seemed to accept that I was looking for a different kind of future.

'You told us to reach for the stars, Sir,' I reminded him.

'Yes, yes I did,' Mr Brown said with a sigh. 'Well, leave it with me, young man. If you're serious, I'll see what I can do.'

And that's how I got to be general dogsbody at the

planetarium, for my work experience week. Sometimes I had to help out in the cafe and sometimes in the galleries. I got to collect tickets and show class groups into the planetarium itself, and I even got to help the guy who runs the star show, which was seriously awesome.

I asked a whole lot of questions too – I talked to the cafe ladies, the security guard, the cleaners, everyone. Nobody minded. When Mr Brown turned up towards the end of the week to assess my progress, he got glowing reports from everybody.

'I'm sorry I doubted you, Mouse,' he said. 'You've been a credit to the school, this week.'

'Thank you, Sir,' I said.

Well, I wasn't about to tell him the real reason I wanted to be there, was I?

You don't get stars on the Eden Estate, where I live.

I know they're up there, beyond the neon-orange glow of the night, but it's not like you can see them. The only sparkle you get around here is the glint of broken glass in the gutter. A place like the Eden Estate makes it hard to believe in magic.

In a place like this, when you find something that really shines, you hang on to it.

That's kind of how I feel about my girlfriend, Cat. She has honey-coloured skin and corkscrew curls and slanting green eyes that shimmer when she smiles. She is pretty and confident and cool. She's a girl who has everything, I guess.

Me, I'm just a skinny kid with a dipping fringe and a talent for trouble; a boy from the Eden Estate. When Cat barged into my life a few months back, she turned everything upside-down. It was like someone switching on the light after years and years of mooching around in the shadows, and there's no going back.

We've had some great times, some scary times, some sad times . . . but we came through all of it, me and Cat.

And today . . . well, today is Cat's birthday.

What do you give to the girl who has everything? Something special, something unique, something out of this world. Something that won't cost much more than the £3.50 I have in the pocket of my skinny jeans.

I've been planning it for ages, seriously.

My little dog, Lucky, tilts his head to one side, his ears askew. 'You can't come,' I tell him. 'Sorry.'

Lucky watches as I pull on a hoodie, rake a comb through my hair. Dogs are not allowed where we're going, but then again . . . well, it wouldn't be a party without him.

'C'mon then, pal,' I say. 'Let's go . . .'

'So,' Cat says as we jump off the Docklands Light Railway at Cutty Sark, with Lucky running on ahead. 'We're going to see where you did your work experience?'

'Thought you'd like it,' I say. 'It's pretty cool.'

Cat looks at her watch. 'Haven't we left it a bit

late, though?' she asks. 'It's getting dark. Surely the planetarium will be closing, soon?'

'We've got time,' I tell her. 'Besides, we couldn't go earlier, your parents were taking you out for lunch. . .'

'I know,' Cat says. 'Sorry, Mouse. I have to be home by ten too . . . they're still being super-strict.'

'No worries. I'll get you back, I promise.'

We walk along the river, watching the boats, dodging the families heading home after a Saturday in Greenwich. Lucky trots ahead, his tail waving in the air.

'There's just one problem,' I say. 'Dogs aren't allowed . . .'

Cat laughs, scooping Lucky up and into her bag. He peers out through the handles like he's used to the celebrity life. 'Keep your head down,' I whisper. 'You're going to land us in trouble!'

Cat ties a pink skull-print scarf to the bag's handle, which helps to hide the fact that there's a dog in there. We head into the building.

'Mouse,' the guy at the door greets me. 'Couldn't stay away, huh?'

'I wanted to show my girlfriend,' I say.

'Better hurry then. We're closing up soon. You've missed the last star show . . .'

Cat looks stricken. 'Was that my birthday treat?' she asks. 'Oh, I'm sorry, Mouse! That would have been so, so cool . . .'

I bite my lip. 'I must have remembered the times

4

wrong,' I say. We wander into the gift shop, and I buy Cat a packet full of hundreds of tiny silver-star sprinkles. 'Not as good as the real thing, but better than nothing. And we can have an ice cream while we're here. . .'

'My own personal universe,' Cat grins, taking the packet of stars. 'That's cool. Thanks, Mouse!'

We sit in the cafe eating ice-cream sundaes, which the lady behind the counter has made specially with strawberries and chocolate sauce and sprinkled nuts. We feed the wafers to Lucky and hope that nobody else can see the black and white tail swishing about just above the top of the bag.

'Sorry I messed it up, Cat,' I say. 'I wanted your birthday to be perfect, not just ice cream by the river. It's not quite what I planned –'

'Doesn't matter!' Cat grins. 'I'm with you, and I'm with Lucky. I have a pocketful of stars . . . besides, we have ice cream! Ice cream and dreams, who needs anything else?'

But the cafe is closing up, chairs are being stacked, tables wiped. A loudspeaker informs us that the building will close in fifteen minutes. I sigh.

'We should just go,' I say, taking Cat's hand. 'I think we can get out this way . . .' I lead her along the corridor, away from the main door. I look around, take a deep breath, then open a storeroom door and pull Cat inside.

Lucky starts to whimper in the darkness. 'What's going on?' Cat yelps. 'This isn't an exit!'

'Shhh!' I hiss. 'It's all part of the plan!'

'The plan?' Cat echoes.

So I explain.

'It's an adventure,' Cat whispers, kissing my nose in the darkness of the storeroom. 'A birthday adventure. Thanks, Mouse!'

In the corridor outside, I can hear the curators and the cafe ladies laughing, chatting, saying goodnight. Then it's quieter, and I know that the security guard will be checking everything, setting the alarms, locking up.

'Won't there be cleaners?' Cat whispers.

'Not till Monday morning,' I explain.

I switch on my torch. There's a big star map on the wall of the storeroom, a black chart with little white stars printed on to it to mark out the constellations. Cat takes a silver marker pen from her bag and draws on a new star, then another, and another. We are a brand-new constellation of three: the Cat Star, the Mouse Star and the Lucky Star.

When I open the storeroom door, the whole place is in darkness. Lucky runs in circles, glad to be free, and Cat turns a cartwheel in the torchlight, laughing. I grab her hand and lead her along the corridor to the theatre, a circular room with a huge domed roof.

I switch on the power, set up the projector, hoping I've remembered it all properly, then sit down with Cat in the darkness, Lucky on my knee. I hand her a Mars bar and a can of Coke, lean back and take her hand in mine. 'I wanted to make your birthday special,' I tell her. 'We're going on a trip around the universe . . .'

'Wow,' says Cat. 'Just you and me and Lucky – and about a million stars!'

The show begins.

We lean back, looking up at the domed ceiling, and suddenly we are hurtling through the swirling blackness, hearts thumping.

A recorded voice guides us through our voyage, explaining how a star is born, how it grows, how it dies. Lucky shifts around, wide-eyed, wagging his tail.

I've seen the star show already, of course, but this time is different. There are no sticky-fingered seven-year-olds, no eagle-eyed teachers, no foreign tourists trying to take photos of the stars. It's just Cat and Lucky and me. We could almost be in our own personal star-ship, heading straight for a whole new universe, or stretched out on a magic carpet, wide-eyed, drifting through solar systems a million miles from home.

As we watch, the star show whirls around us, scoops us up and lifts us high . . . away from reality, away from our worries, and far, far away from the Eden Estate. We swoop and soar beyond the earth, beyond the sun, out into the velvet darkness – free.

The three of us would have stayed in that planetarium forever, running the star show over and over, but Cat is on a curfew. She has to be home by ten, and I promised to get her there.

I switch off the projector and tuck the last Mars bar beneath it, by way of a thank you. Cat adds a sprinkle of tiny silver stars, and I smile, wondering what the star show guy will make of it on Monday.

We make our escape through the window of the Ladies Toilets, closing it gently behind us. Cat leaves a scattering of silver stars on the ground where we land, and then we're running, laughing, hand in hand, Lucky sprinting on ahead.

We stop beside the river to catch our breath, still grinning. The whole of London is spread out before us, a glittering skyline of neon lights and towering rooftops. Even the river boats are lit up now, gliding across the dark, glossy Thames.

'It was the best birthday ever,' Cat is saying. 'The star show was awesome . . . a trip around the Milky Way. How cool?'

'When I leave school, I'd like to work there for real,' I say. 'Studying the stars, working the projector, helping kids to see that there's magic out there, if you know where to look . . .'

'We could see the star show whenever we want,' Cat breathes. 'But, Mouse . . . nothing could ever beat tonight. It was an adventure, and it was cool, and it was also the most romantic thing anyone's ever done for me . . .'

I slide an arm round her shoulder and the two of us look up towards the clear night sky, Lucky wagging his tail at our feet. As we watch, a bright silver star falls down through the darkness, trailing a blur of white behind it.

I look at Cat's face, her mouth open in a perfect 'o', her eyes wide, and I laugh because you can't plan everything, and sometimes the unexpected things are the best of all.

'Make a wish!' Cat whispers.

Right now, though, I have just about everything in the world that I could want, and wishing for more would just be plain greedy. Cat flings her arms round my neck and hugs me, and then we're kissing, softly, under a sky of stars.

If you'd like to read more about Cat and Mouse, check out Cathy Cassidy's new book Lucky Star, *out now in paperback . . .*

Super Starry Facts

When we look up at the stars, we are **looking back in time**! The light that we see shining from the stars in the sky can be millions, or even billions, of years old!

The closer a star is to the **Earth's horizon**, the more it appears to **twinkle**.

There are **more stars in the universe** than there are grains of sand on all the beaches in the world.

If you could put **Saturn** in an enormous bathtub, **it would float**!

The amazing streaks of light that we know as **shooting stars** are in fact **meteors** falling into the Earth's atmosphere and burning up. Doesn't stop us wishing on them, though!

A **teaspoonful of neutron star** would weigh about 112 million tonnes.

And the best fact of all . . .

we are all made of stardust!

What's in Your Stars?

Some people believe that the position of the stars at the time of a person's birth can affect their character. How well do you and your friends fit your star signs? Match your birthdays to the descriptions below and see.

There's some space under each sign to write down friends who fall into each category – try to find one friend for each sign. Maybe it will help you to understand each other even better than you already do!

Aries

Birthday: 21 March – 20 April
Symbol: 'The Ram' ★ **Element: Fire**
You're full of energy, very determined and you rarely let anything stand in your way, making you a brilliant leader and organizer. You're competitive and like to be the best, and you can sometimes have a hot temper if you don't get your way. But because you're so friendly, kind and generous, you're an absolutely brilliant mate to have.
Celebrity Arians: Keira Knightley and Emma Watson

My Arian friend: ....

Taurus

Birthday: 21 April – 21 May
Symbol: 'The Bull' ★ **Element:** Earth

Friends don't come more loyal than you! You're patient, reliable and incredibly trustworthy – what you see is what you get! You like being in your comfort zone, and you're not a big risk taker – but far from being stuck in your ways, you're very creative and artistic, which makes you great fun to be around.

Celebrity Taureans: Kirsten Dunst and Lily Allen

My Taurean friend: ....

Gemini

Birthday: 22 May – 21 June
Symbol: 'The Twins' ★ **Element:** Air

Geminis are impulsive, energetic and always on the move. You HATE being bored, and too much relaxation drives you crazy. Life is never dull when you're around! You can be quite hard to pin down, but when it comes to friends you're extremely affectionate, and you're never stuck for a good joke!

Celebrity Geminis: Kylie Minogue and Cathy Cassidy

My Gemini friend: ....

Cancer

Birthday: 22 June – 23 July
Symbol: 'The Crab' ★ **Element:** Water

Cancerians often have great memories, and tend to be interested in history and collecting things. You sometimes pretend to be tough, but it's all an act – you're really emotional, sensitive and giving, and your friends value you as a great listener.

Celebrity Cancerians: Lindsay Lohan and Daniel Radcliffe

My Cancerian friend: ....

Leo

Birthday: 24 July – 23 August
Symbol: 'The Lion' ★ **Element: Fire**

You're larger than life, full of energy and ideas, and you're not afraid to be the centre of attention. You're the life and soul of every party! People love to be around you because you're so much fun, and you're incredibly generous towards your friends and family. But watch out for that lion's temper!

Celebrity Leos: Madonna and Jennifer Lopez

My Leo friend: ....

Virgo

Birthday: 24 August – 23 September
Symbol: 'The Virgin' ★ **Element: Earth**

Virgos often feel misunderstood. You find it hard to be open with your feelings, and like to express yourself through actions, rather than words. You're incredibly organized and always know what to do in a crisis, which makes you a brilliant friend to have around. And although it takes a while to get to know you, you're gentle, kind and have a great sense of humour.

Celebrity Virgos: Billie Piper and Rachel Bilson

My Virgo friend: ....

Libra

Birthday: 24 September – 23 October
Symbol: 'The Scales' ★ **Element: Air**

You like to please people and surround yourself with friends. You really hate feeling unwanted! You're not a decision maker – you'd rather just go with the flow and let your mates sort things out. You tend to get on with everyone, and people like to be around you because you're easy-going, affectionate and sympathetic.

Celebrity Librans: Zac Efron and Sharon Osbourne

My Libran friend: ....

Scorpio

Birthday: 24 October – 22 November
Symbol: 'The Scorpion' ★ **Element: Water**

You're extremely intelligent and like to be in control of things. Nothing escapes your notice, and if anyone crosses you, they better watch out – you don't hold back on how you feel! You're very loyal to your friends, and you like to see the same in return. To those you love, you're gentle, kind-hearted and caring.

Celebrity Scorpios: Scarlett Johansson and Brittany Murphy

My Scorpian friend: ....

Sagittarius

Birthday: 23 November – 21 December
Symbol: 'The Centaur' ★ **Element: Fire**

You're fun-loving, generous and super-friendly, so people love you! Honesty is always your policy – you say what you think and never ever fib. Sometimes your bluntness can make people feel uncomfortable, but you always mean well. You're open-minded and interested in everything, so people find you very approachable and comforting. You're a big fan of hugging, and like to know that you're loved.

Celebrity Sagittarians: Katie Holmes and Kelly Brook

My Sagittarian friend: ....

Capricorn

Birthday: 22 December – 20 January
Symbol: 'The Goat' ★ **Element: Earth**

You're reliable, practical and you tend to take life seriously – althoug you're also known for your dry, witty sense of humour. Confrontation upsets you – when things get tough, you like to try and keep the pea and you're usually able to charm even the most difficult of people. You're creative, sensitive and kind, and great at keeping secrets, so your friends really trust you and talk to you about everything.

Celebrity Capricorns: James McAvoy and Kate Moss

My Capricorn friend: ....

Aquarius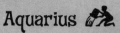

Birthday: 21 January – 19 February
Symbol: 'The Water Bearer' ★ **Element: Air**

As an Aquarius, you're clever, super-friendly, original and very inventive. People often comment on your unusual and creative dress sense! You're pretty sure of yourself, and you know a thing or two about most subjects, but you're always up for learning something new too. You're also very patient, so you're great at helping mates with their homework!

Celebrity Aquarians: Jennifer Aniston and Mischa Barton

My Aquarian friend: ....

Pisces

Birthday: 20 February – 20 March
Symbol: 'The Fish' ★ **Element: Water**

Creativity is your thing! You're clever and resourceful and always thinking outside the box. You're a great dreamer, so sometimes you're accused of having your head in the clouds. But when it comes to friendship there's no one more thoughtful and caring, and you see the best in everyone.

Celebrity Pisceans: Dakota Fanning and Rihanna

My Piscean friend: ....

Star-maker!

Put some sparkle in your lives with these starry makes …

Wrap Stars

Print your own cool gift wrap - easy!

★ Cut a small, uncooked potato in half.

★ Draw a star shape on the surface and carefully use a knife to trim away the flesh around the sides so you are left with a star-shaped printing block.

★ Let the spud dry out for an hour or so, then paint the surface with gold/silver poster paint and start printing!

★ Test your prints out on newspaper and when you've got the knack, move on to sheets of dark blue or black tissue paper.

Seriously cool gift wrap …

Star Fruit!

Star fruit are delicious and when you slice them, they make a gorgeous star shape. You can add them to your pizza instead of pineapple, include them in fruit salads for an exotic touch or make a delicious Star Fruit Smoothie!

Star Fruit Smoothie

75g plain yoghurt
80ml fresh orange juice
1 large star fruit
1 mango, peeled and de-stoned

★ Put all of the ingredients in a blender and blend until smooth.

★ Pour the smoothie into a tall glass and top off with slices of star fruit round the rim of the glass.

16

Shine on . . .

Personalize writing paper, envelopes, notebooks, etc. with cute star prints.

- Recycle your little brother's plasticine to make a printing block.

- Squidge the plasticine into a small star shape, then press against a hard surface to flatten the star.

- Brush with glittery poster paint and get decorating!

Card prints are cool too.

- Cut a piece of card 1cm x 3cm and use the long edge to print a line.

- Print another line across it to make a cross shape, then another two diagonally across those to make a star shape . . . cool!

- Use with fabric paint to print dinky stars along the hem of last year's T-shirt!

3D Stars

- Draw two identical stars on stiff paper and cut them out.

- Decorate the stars with coloured pens, glitter and foil.

- Take the first star and cut a slit from the end of one point into the middle of the star, and then take the second star and cut a slit from between two points into the middle of the star.

- Slot your two stars together and you have a twinkling 3D star that you can put on your book shelves or your window sill, or hang from your ceiling.

Could YOU be a STAR?

Have you got the sparkle to really shine?
Find out with our fun quiz!

1) You're spending a whole Saturday with your friends. You:

a) Splash out and be waterbabes for the day, getting fit and checking out the cute lads at the local pool.

b) Hit the shops, trying on the poshest dresses you can find. After all, one day you'll be rich and famous . . .

c) Hang out at the skate park, listening to cool music on your iPod and hoping nobody offers you a go on their skateboard!

d) Plan a day full of fun, with something each of your mates will like – if they're happy, you're happy.

2) You're feeling low. How do you handle it?

a) Go for a long run or cycle ride to take your mind off it – exercise always cheers you up.

b) Pretend nothing's wrong. Act like you're happy, and pretty soon you will be!

c) Hole up in your room listening to loud, gloomy rock tracks – those bands really know how you're feeling.

d) Call your friends and talk things through – between you, you can fix almost anything and beat the blues.

3) Of all your achievements, you're most proud of the time you . . .

a) completed the local mini-marathon in record time.

b) played an angel in the school nativity play!

c) won the karaoke contest on holiday.

d) rescued a kitten from drowning.

4) You've been asked to sign up for an after-school activity. You choose:

a) Netball club . . . it's fun, fast and helps you stay fit, plus you love the competitive bits!

b) The school play. OK, so you're only painting scenery, but you're learning all the lines in case the lead actress drops out!

c) Orchestra. While everyone else is playing the clarinet, you're hammering out an MCR song on the school drum kit . . .

d) The anti-bullying scheme – you want to help other kids get their lives back on track.

Add up your score and find out what kind of star YOU are!

Mostly **A**s:
You're a SPORTS STAR – fit, healthy and bursting with energy! You can be competitive, but you're a good team player too – whatever you set your mind to, you can achieve!

Mostly **B**s:
You're a MOVIE STAR – and any day now, you'll be ready for your red-carpet moment! You love drama, glamour and acting – and not just on the stage. Remember us when you're famous!

Mostly **C**s:
You're a ROCK STAR – cool, funky and not afraid to stand out from the crowd. OK, so today it's recorder lessons and singing in the shower, but tomorrow it'll be centre stage at Glastonbury . . .

Mostly **D**s:
You're a SUPER STAR – you're not looking for fame, fortune, gold medals or red carpets, but you could be the brightest star of all. You're kind, caring and thoughtful – a friend in a million. Go, girl!

So you know Dizzy and Indigo and Scarlett's stories – but what about Cathy's?

Little C

C is for Coventry and camper vans

a is for arts and crafts, agony aunt and advice

t is for teaching and thistles

h is for happiness and Hannah . . . and Paul and Joey and Mouse and Jude and Cat and Ginger – the list of Cathy's fabulous characters is endless!

y is for yummy ice cream and YOU

Cathy was born in **1962** in a place called Coventry in the West Midlands. Cathy was always destined to travel the country with her books in her **bright red camper van** – at the age of eight she wrote her first picture book for her little brother and made comics to sell to her friends!

A few years later, Cathy went to **study art in Liverpool** and then she worked as a fiction editor on the super-famous *Jackie magazine*. Later on, Cathy married her boyfriend, **Liam,** and trained to be an art teacher. After a happy few years teaching in Coventry, Cathy and Liam moved to bonny Scotland to start a family (they have a daughter, **Caitlin,** and a son, **Calum**) and Cathy began writing books. First came the delightful *Dizzy,* then the brilliant *Indigo Blue, Driftwood, Scarlett, Sundae Girl, Lucky Star* and *Ice cream and Dreams*.

Cathy was also the agony aunt for a **teen magazine** until recently, and she absolutely loves writing for, and hearing from, all her amazing fans . . . she couldn't do it without you!

cathy cassidy

tells all

Where do you get the ideas for your stories?

I get ideas from all around me – things I see, hear, read, remember, imagine . . . then I daydream, and sometimes the ideas turn into a story!

What's the best thing about writing stories?

I get to imagine being all kinds of different characters and dream up a million different situations, so life is never dull or boring! It's so cool watching a daydream unfurl on paper . . . and knowing that my readers get to share that daydream is brilliant too!

If you couldn't be a writer, what would you be?

I've been everything from a waitress and petrol-pump attendant to an art teacher and an agony aunt . . . but if I had to start over, I'd run an animal sanctuary or be a craft worker making weird textiley things.

What do you like to do when you aren't writing?

I'm addicted to reading – especially teen books! I also love swimming, eating cake with friends, music festivals, tepee nights and anything arty/crafty.

What advice can you give to aspiring writers?

1. Read lots – you'll learn all about plot, style and dialogue as you go.
2. Write – practise, practise, practise – then practise some more!
3. Write about what you care about – it'll show in your work.
4. Carry a notebook to jot down ideas/thoughts.
5. Daydream. It's free exercise for the imagination – all of my stories start off that way!

And now for the crucial quick fire-questions:

What's your favourite . . .

Cathy as
a teenag

COLOUR? Moss green

WORD? Chocolate (sigh . . .)

ANIMAL? Llama (but donkeys and hares are cool too!)

PLACE IN THE WORLD?
Either the Galloway hills or the west coast of Ireland, but Sri Lanka is awesome too . . .

NUMBER? Don't have one – I'm allergic to numbers!

BOOK? *The Catcher in the Rye* by J. D. Salinger, a fab American teen book from the 50s . . . but I have a million fave books, so it's hard to choose just one!

Ginger Snaps

Turn over for an EXCLUSIVE sneak preview of Cathy's amazing new story coming in July

I keep an eye on Emily Croft, and I don't like what I see. All week, she is alone – in class, at break, at lunchtime. Now she's in the school canteen, hunched over a plate of macaroni, looking like someone just shot her pet hamster. She's starting to get that loser look, all drab and dull and defeated.

'There's Emily,' I say to Shannon as we pay for our lunches. 'On her own again.'

Shannon frowns. 'I feel sorry for her,' she says. 'But . . .'

Yeah, exactly. But.

As we edge past with our laden trays, Emily looks up and catches my eye, as if to remind me of the times at primary school when I was glad of her company. 'OK, Emily?' I ask.

She smiles, but the smile is too thin. On impulse, I turn back, dipping my tray down to the tabletop. 'Any room here?' I ask. 'Can we join you?'

Shannon raises an eyebrow, but Emily's face lights up, and we sit down. *Random acts of kindness*, I think, like Sam Taylor said. The world needs more of them.

'So,' I say. 'How's it going?'

'Oh, you know,' Emily says. 'I'm OK.'

There's a pause, a long, empty moment when nobody knows quite what to say. We're waiting for Emily to smile and nod and steer the conversation on to safer ground, but she has other ideas. Her lower lip quivers and her eyes brim with tears.

'It's just so awful having to do everything alone,' she blurts, looking at me with feeling, as though she's only just sussed what I went through every day of primary school. Well, maybe she has.

'You'll make new friends,' Shannon says, sounding irritated.

Emily sighs. 'I suppose. Everyone has their friends already, though. It's hard to break into a new group.'

What am I supposed to say to that? OK, no problem, have my friends? I don't think so.

Shannon leans across the table, twisting a strand of golden-blonde hair between her fingers. 'You know what, Emily?' she says, narrowing her big blue eyes. 'You have to stop feeling sorry for yourself. Your best friend's gone – well, tough. You'll never find a new one if you dissolve into tears every time someone comes near you.'

'Shannon!' I say, shocked.

Emily blinks. 'No, no,' she says. 'Shannon's right. I'm pathetic, right?'

'Kind of,' Shannon says.

'You're not!' I protest, but Emily is dabbing her eyes, sitting up straighter. The ghost of a smile flickers across her face.

'No, no, I needed to hear that,' she says in a small, steely voice. 'I need to let go, move on. Well, OK, fine. I'll do that. Thanks, Shannon.'

Thanks, Shannon? Huh?

'No more crying either,' Shannon says. 'It makes your eyes all piggy and bloodshot. Not a good look.'

'Got you,' Emily says, taking a long breath in. 'Sorry.'

Shannon just shrugs and smiles. 'Any time,' she says.

'Poor Emily,' Shannon says later, as we're getting changed for netball. 'She really hasn't got a clue, has she?'

Emily is already in her PE kit, bright-eyed and

smiling, handing out tie-on netball bibs for Miss Jackson. She's so eager to please it's just plain embarrassing.

'She's trying,' I shrug.

'Very trying,' Shannon quips. 'I'm glad you got us to sit with her at lunch, though. I mean, I do feel sorry for her, and if she's an old friend of yours . . .'

'Not a friend exactly,' I say. 'She was just a girl in my class . . .'

'Well, whatever,' Shannon decides. 'It doesn't matter. We'll be nice to her, yeah? Watch out for her.'

'OK,' I agree, although I'm not sure that Shannon's tough-love style of being nice is exactly what Emily needs. Maybe – maybe not.

'Darn, I can't find my trainers . . .' I turn my rucksack upside down, rooting through the books and pens and sweet wrappers. Nothing. Too late, I remember dumping them in my locker on the first day of term.

'Miss Jackson,' I say. 'I've left my trainers in my locker . . . can I run and get them?'

'Be quick then,' the PE teacher replies. 'We'll be out on the netball courts, warming up.'

'I'll be two minutes,' I promise.

I head out into the silent corridors, conspicuous in a grey wraparound netball skirt, stripy socks and T-shirt. I open my locker, dig out the trainers and sit down on a bench to put them on. Out of nowhere a few lockers down from me, new boy Sam Taylor appears, struggling to extract a large tattered brown suitcase.

'Hey, Ginger Snaps,' he says, grinning at me from under the trilby hat, and I smile in spite of myself. 'Nice skirt. Very . . . ' He narrows his eyes, struggling to find the right word.

'Short?' I suggest.

'I'm not complaining,' Sam says. 'I think you may be pushing the uniform rules a bit today, but who am I to point the finger? Besides, it's very, very cute.'

I smile. 'I'm not pushing the school uniform rules,' I say. 'It's my PE kit. Shouldn't you have PE too?'

Sam Taylor frowns, considering. 'Ah,' he says. 'Football, I think. I knew there was something . . .'

Silence falls between us, awkward and heavy, broken only by a tinny, clanking sound as he pulls out the big brown case and slams the locker door. The suitcase is ancient, the corners patched with parcel tape, the clasps long since broken. A leather belt, wrapped around it, is all that is keeping it closed.

'What have you got in there?' I ask him. 'Don't tell me: footy boots, ball, collapsible goalposts?'

'Not exactly.' He unhooks the belt, opens the case and lifts out a saxophone – a big golden, shiny curve of metal – from its bed of black velvet. He clips on the neck and the mouthpiece, slips the strap over his head and turns to me, cradling it like a small child. 'Like it?'

I blink. 'I didn't know you were musical!' I accuse.

'There's lots you don't know about me,' Sam shrugs, and it sounds like a challenge. Suddenly, I'd like to know everything there is to know about Sam Taylor.

'I'm in a band,' he explains. 'Ska Tissue. We play ska music.'

'Ska music?'

'It's from the late seventies, a kind of mixture of jazz and soul and reggae with a bit of punk thrown in. Very upbeat and cool. Trilby hats were part of the look.'

'That figures,' I say. 'Who else is in the band then?'

Sam looks thoughtful. 'Well, I play sax,

obviously,' he tells me. 'We have a vacancy for guitar, bass, drums and keyboard at the moment. Oh, and vocals. We're just starting out.'

I bite back a smile. 'Let me get this straight,' I say. 'You're in a band, but there are no other members?'

'Not yet,' Sam admits. 'Can you sing?'

Shannon is right – this boy is weird – hopelessly, gloriously weird. I start walking away. 'No,' I tell him over my shoulder. 'I can't sing.'

'Too bad.'

Suddenly, an ear-splitting burst of sax music fills the corridor behind me. It's loud and jazzy and upbeat and cool, making the air around me sing. It's the kind of music that makes you smile, like it or not.

Unless you're Mr Kelly, that is. The maths teacher storms out of his classroom up ahead of me, purple-faced. 'Sam Taylor!' he roars. 'Stop that this minute!'

Maybe Sam can't stop right away, though. It's probably something to do with breath and timing and lung capacity, because the music goes on louder than ever – crazy, happy sounds that bounce off the grey corridor walls and dance along the scratchy nylon carpet beneath my feet. It finally squeals to a halt as I push through the double doors that lead out towards the netball courts.

'Do you know,' I say to Shannon when I find her, 'that a wraparound netball skirt can be very, very cute?'

'Are you crazy?' Shannon asks. 'A netball skirt is a crime against fashion. It's like a couple of grey tea towels with pleats. Cute? I don't think so.'

I just smile.

We win our netball match six goals to two. Predictably, Emily Croft scores three of them. Miss Jackson blows the whistle and we troop back up to the changing rooms. As we cross the playground, the Year Eight boys are straggling up from football.

Sam Taylor made it in the end, obviously. He's at the back in a mud-spattered footy kit, still wearing his hat.

Best Friends Forever!

Some people say that money makes the world go round. Others say it's love that keeps us spinning. But if Cathy Cassidy's books are anything to go by, then friendship is the most important thing of all (and maybe a nice dollop of ice cream too!). Everyone needs a best friend to help them through the difficult times, and to make the most of the good ones – just look at Cat and Mouse.

Turn over for some fab tips on how to hold your very own brilliant Friendship Festival, plus some lovely things to make and do with your own best mates.

Great Mates . . .

- Are there for each other, good times or bad.
- Can keep a secret!
- Have fun! Go skating, dancing, shopping, swimming, cycling . . . whatever does it for you!
- Understand the healing power of chocolate!
- Would never let a boy come between them.
- Know that bullying/bitching are sad and uncool.
- Can talk to each other about anything.
- Trust each other.
- Aren't scared to tell you when you're wrong . . .
- Share dreams, T-shirts, cake . . . and Cathy Cassidy books!
- Rock!

33

Friendship Festivals:

One of the coolest things about being a published author is getting the chance to meet my readers! Forget the flash car, the only thing I really wanted to buy with my advance was a VW camper van! It's fab to take it to bookshops, libraries, schools and festivals, and that's how the Cathy Cassidy Friendship Festival evolved.

A friendship festival is all about having fun – and making new friends! There's always plenty to do – quizzes, hair-braiding, friendship bracelets, face-painting . . . and music and munchies, of course! Friendship is something worth celebrating, so why not use these ideas to put on your own Friendship Festival . . . go for it!

Cathy Cassidy
x

Getting ready:

- Send all your friends an invitation telling them where and when the Friendship Festival is happening

- You could ask everyone to dress up for the event and maybe award a prize for the best outfit

On the day:

- Set the scene by decorating the venue with brightly coloured streamers and balloons.

- Announce the start of the Friendship Festival and explain how Cathy tours the country with her van.

- Gather everyone together and read a chapter from one of Cathy's books.

- Friendship bracelets are great fun to make. All you need to do is buy some brightly coloured thread and then plait three strings together. It's easier if you work in pairs and get a bit of adult help to start you off.

- There are lots of other things you can do to make your Friendship Festival really special, such as hair-braiding, funky music, make-overs, hand-/face-painting, nail art, T-shirt customizing, drinks and munchies, competitions, sleepovers, henna tattoos and lots of other craft activities (e.g. making bookmarks out of thread and beads).

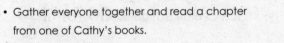

Have fun!

Ice-cream Heaven!

Make your own **delicious** ice cream sundaes. Go for it!

Scrummy Strawberry Sundae

Fresh strawberries
2 wafers
Strawberry sauce
Vanilla ice cream

1 Finely chop the fresh strawberries and mix half of them with the ice cream in a bowl.

2 Layer scoops of the ice cream and strawberry mixture with the remaining chopped strawberries and strawberry sauce in tall glasses.

3 Top with a wafer, a drizzle of strawberry sauce and a juicy strawberry. Yum!

Did you know?

The average number of licks needed to polish off a single scoop ice-cream cone is approximately 50.

Marshmallow Madness!

Raspberry or
black cherry jam

Chocolate ice cream

Marshmallows

Squirty cream

Glacé cherries (optional)

Chopped nuts (optional)

1 Put two spoonfuls of jam into the bottom of a pretty glass.

2 Add a scoop of chocolate ice cream on top.

3 Chop up the marshmallows and sprinkle them on top of the ice cream, saving some for later.

4 Add a layer of squishy squirty cream.

5 Sprinkle with the chopped nuts and top the sundae with two cherries and more chopped marshmallows.

Did you know?

One of the biggest ice-cream sundaes ever made was 3.7 metres high! It took 17,667 litres of ice cream and 3,175 kilograms of toppings.

Chocolate Heaven!

3 chocolate chip cookies, crumbled
4 squares of chocolate, grated
Vanilla ice cream
Chocolate ice cream
Chocolate sauce
Squirty cream

1 In a tall glass, layer a scoop of vanilla ice cream and a sprinkle of crumbled cookie.

2 Then add a scoop of chocolate ice cream and a layer of grated chocolate.

3 Add another scoop of vanilla ice cream and a layer of crumbled cookie.

4 Top with a layer of squishy squirty cream and decorate with grated chocolate and sauce . . . bliss!

Did you know?

The most popular flavour by far is vanilla, followed by chocolate, strawberry and Neapolitan.

Peanut Butter and Banana Sundae

Crunchy peanut butter
Plain frozen yoghurt
1 banana
Honey

1 In a bowl, mix the crunchy peanut butter and frozen yoghurt.

2 Put a scoop of the peanut butter and ice-cream mixture into an ice-cream bowl.

3 Sprinkle some slices of banana over the top and add another scoop of peanut butter and ice cream.

4 Drizzle honey over the top, and add some more slices of banana.

5 For an extra treat, top with some chunks of chocolate or marshmallows.

Create your own ice-cream sundae!

With a couple of flavours of ice cream, sorbet or frozen yoghurt, you can create your own yummy sundaes.

Cathy Cassidy's
My Best Friend Rocks
competition is a fab way to show your friend that you think she's the best friend ever!

Here is last year's winner, Rebecca, talking about the award and why she nominated her best friend, Emma.

Rebecca, what made you nominate your friend Emma?

I nominated Emma because we have been best friends since we were four years old and have always been there for each other. Two years ago I realized just how good a friend she was when my mum was diagnosed with cancer. She helped me through some really hard times and even joined me in running the Race for Life that year! I wanted to give her something back as I will never be able to thank her enough for what she has done for me.

How did you feel when you found out that you were one of the finalists?

When we found out we were one of the six finalists I couldn't believe it. I immediately rang Emma and she was as shocked as me. I was so happy that I entered because now Emma knows how much I appreciate her as my friend.

Tell us about the award ceremony and the moment Cathy called out your names as the winners.

The awards ceremony was fantastic! We were made to feel really special the second we walked through the door. After having some smoothies and some delicious food while meeting Cathy Cassidy and the other girls, we started the awards ceremony. Cathy talked us through all of the entries and how we all deserved to win. Then the moment came when she announced the winners and when she called out our names it was like a dream. We were so happy. After that we received our prizes and had lots of pictures taken to put in Mizz.

Your prize was everything you need for the sleepover of your dreams. Have you had the sleepover?

We've had a sleepover and it was great! It took place at Emma's house. We did makeovers on each other, using the make-up and hair straighteners that we got. And then did our own mini photo shoot, which Emma's sister Laura helped us with. We also had a really great time spending the vouchers we got. The DVDs we bought with the HMV vouchers we got came in handy at the sleepover too!

What do you think makes a good friendship?

I think a good friendship needs trust and honesty. You have to look out for each other and be there for each other through good times and bad, just like Emma was there for me.

What's your favourite Cathy Cassidy book?

All of Cathy Cassidy's books are brilliant but I think if I had to choose one it would be *Indigo Blue* because it was the first ever Cathy Cassidy book I read and it really stuck in my mind. I think I read it in about two days because I couldn't put it down. I would recommend any of the Cathy Cassidy books to anyone, but most of all *Indigo Blue*.

Find out how to nominate your friend for this year's My Best Friend Rocks competition at cathycassidy.com NOW!

FRIENDS
try our fun quiz to see

1) Your best friend suddenly seems moody and troubled. You:
a) Ask her quietly what's wrong.
b) Plan a special treat – involving lots of chocolate! – to take her mind off things.
c) Play her favourite CD at full blast – it's bound to cheer her up!

2) You and your mate have a huge crush on the same person. You:
a) Are honest about how you feel and remind her how important friendship is. If it's going to hurt one of you, maybe it's not worth it . . .
b) Feel jealous, but pretend nothing is wrong.
c) Check out his also-very-cute best mate instead!

3) One of your friends is having problems at home. You:
a) Encourage her to tell a teacher or call a helpline.
b) Get her to confide in you and try to work out a solution.
c) Make her a special friendship bracelet to show your support. Peace and love make everything better!

forever?
how you rate as a mate

4) **You had a great idea for a school event, but your best friend is stealing all the glory. You:**

a) Tell her you're really pleased she's so enthusiastic about your idea, and that you're looking forward to all the fun of working together on it.

b) Write it off as experience, and keep coming up with fab ideas!

c) Feel proud of her for pushing your idea and helping to make it happen.

5) **You catch your best friend's boyfriend kissing someone else. You:**

a) Tell her gently what you've seen, and let her cry on your shoulder.

b) Warn her boyfriend that he'd better start behaving. You'll definitely dish the dirt next time.

c) Break the news sensitively and then throw a fab girls-only sleepover. Who needs boyfriends anyway!

6) **You've rowed with your best friend and fallen out. You:**

a) Forget about it after five minutes and give her a hug to make up. It was a silly fight, and friends don't hold grudges!

b) Try to patch things up, whether it was your fault or not.

c) Blame yourself – steer clear of her for a while and hope that a bit of love, peace and chocolate can sort it all out!

TURN OVER ➡

cathycassidy.com

Now add up your score and see what kind of friend you are!

Mostly As:

*You're **kind, caring, thoughtful** and **fun**. You're a **good listener** and friends often tell you their troubles – you're one of life's unofficial agony aunts/uncles, and a really **brilliant** mate.*

Mostly Bs:

*You're a **good** friend – most of the time! You can be **insecure** and you don't always know the best way to handle a problem, but you're a fun, **loyal friend** all the same.*

Mostly Cs:

*You're **bright, lively** and do things your own way – friendship included! You're a **true friend** and **fun** to have around, though not always as **sensitive** as you could be when a mate's in trouble. Remember that good friends take time to listen too!*

cathycassidy.com

The Cathy Cassidy
Friendship Quiz!

Think you know your best friend better than they know themselves?
Fill in our fab quiz and find out! It's really easy – just write **YOUR**
answers to the questions below, and then – **NO PEEKING** – turn
over and ask your friend to answer the same questions too!
Then turn back and see how many of your answers are the same.

And remember – no sneaky peeking!

SIDE ONE

My name is

....

My favourite flavour of ice cream is

....

The most rebellious thing I've ever done is

....

If I had to choose ONE song to go on my MP3 player, it would be

....

My hero is

....

My greatest ambition is

....

My name is

....

My best mate's name is

....

Their favourite flavour of ice cream is

....

The most rebellious thing they've ever done is

....

If they had to choose ONE song to go on
their MP3 player, it would be

....

Their hero is

....

Their greatest ambition is

....

NOW you can peek!
Time to see how well you really know each other!

FRIENDSHIP NOTEBOOK

Use this gorgeous friendship notebook to make sure you have a record of your best friends FOR EVER!

Fill in the first page about yourself and add a photo. Then give it to your friends to fill in a page each and you'll have a friendship notebook to treasure for ever.

Bessie Mates

My Name

....

Birthday

....

Star sign

....

Favourite colour

....

Fave Cathy Cassidy character

....

Best sleepover film

....

Favourite music

....

Bessie mate memory

....

....

Friend's Name

....

Birthday

....

Star sign

....

Favourite colour

....

Fave Cathy Cassidy character

....

Best sleepover film

....

Favourite music

....

Bessie mate memory

....

....

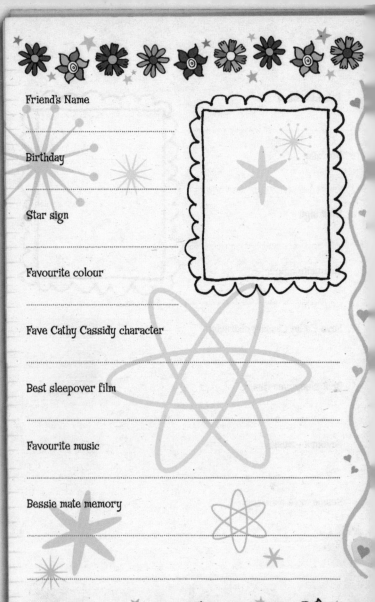

Friend's Name

....

Birthday

....

Star sign

....

Favourite colour

....

Fave Cathy Cassidy character

....

Best sleepover film

....

Favourite music

....

Bessie mate memory

....

....

Friend's Name

....

Birthday

....

Star sign

....

Favourite colour

....

Fave Cathy Cassidy character

....

Best sleepover film

....

Favourite music

....

Bessie mate memory

....

....

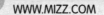

catch all of the latest news and gossip from

cathy cassidy

at

cathycassidy.com

Sneaky peeks at new titles

Details of signings and events near you

Audio extracts and interviews with cathy

post your messages and pictures

Don't miss a word!

Sign up to receive a FREE email newsletter from Cathy into your Inbox every month

Go to cathycassidy.com
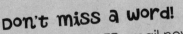

Follow your dreams
with all
cathy cassidy's
gorgeous books

Exclusive news . . .
Coming in July 2008
Cathy's amazing new story

Ginger Snaps

Ever wished you could be someone else?

Gone are the days when **Ginger** was an outsider, always on the fringes of friendship. She's swapped **puppy fat** and **pigtails** for **make-up** and **hair straighteners** and never looked back – until now. Ginger and Shannon are **best mates**, but when they befriend lonely **Emily**, everything changes. Even the **saxophone-playing boy** in the trilby hat can't help – he's part of the problem. Are Ginger and Shannon drifting apart or can they stay best friends forever?

Keep checking
cathycassidy.com
for the latest info and see page 23 for an exclusive sneaky peek.

BEST FRIENDS are there for you in the good times and the bad. They can keep a secret and understand the healing power of chocolate.

BEST FRIENDS make you laugh and make you happy. They are there when things go wrong, and never expect any thanks.

BEST FRIENDS are forever,
BEST FRIENDS ROCK!

cathy cassidy's
My Best Friend Rocks!
enter at
cathycassidy.com

mizz

award

IS YOUR BEST FRIEND ONE IN A MILLION?
Go to **cathycassidy.com**
to find out how you can show your best friend how much you care.

In association with

ChildLine 0800 1111 & **mizz**